THE CHRISTMAS TRAIN

IVAN GANTSCHEV

Long ago and far away there was
a little railway station, where
Vassil the railwayman lived with
his little daughter, Malina.

It was Vassil's job to make sure that the railway line through the mountains was clear and safe for the trains. Falls of rock could happen very suddenly and block the line and cause accidents.

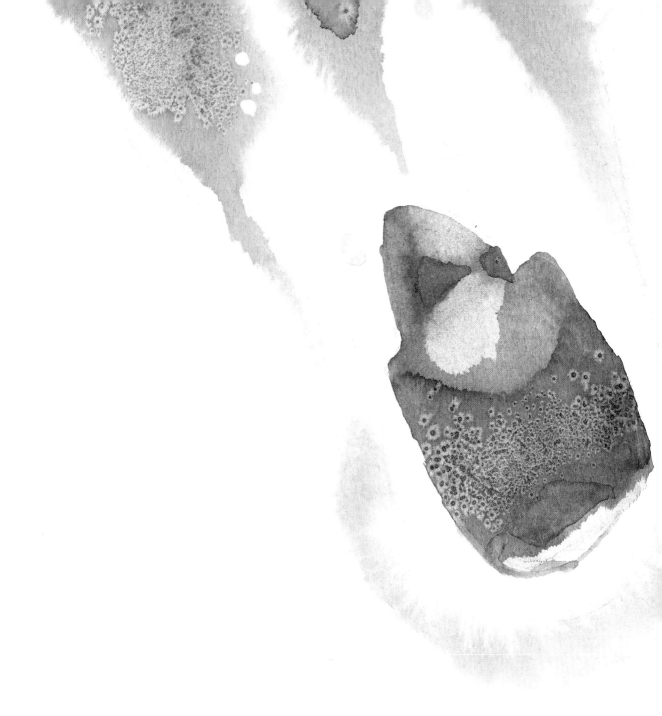

And so, on the afternoon before Christmas Eve, Vassil
was out as usual, working on the railway line. Malina was
busy at home making decorations for the Christmas tree.
She kept thinking about the Christmas present her father
had promised her – what sort of surprise would it be?
She couldn't wait for him to come home and she kept going
to the window to look out for him.

   Suddenly Malina heard a terrible crash like thunder.
Her little dog, Bella, barked and barked and scratched wildly
at the door. "It must be a rockfall," Malina shouted in
horror and she rushed outside to see.

And there, completely blocking the railway track, was a huge heap of rocks. Suddenly, after the loud noise, everything in the mountains was silent and still. Malina was frightened. "The express train will be here in half an hour! What shall I do? I wonder what Daddy would do? I know – I must warn the train driver."

She paused for a moment to think and then ran back home as fast as she could, with Bella bounding along beside her.

Malina remembered what her father had told her
time and time again, "If the line is blocked then
find a place 400 metres in front of the accident, light
a fire and wave a lamp to and fro to warn the train
driver so that he has plenty of time to brake."

Malina tugged at the Christmas tree and carried it
out of the house. She didn't even notice as all the
pretty decorations fell off on to the floor.

She ran down the railway line towards the tunnel,
dragging the Christmas tree behind her. Now
there was only fifteen minutes left before the express
arrived!

The tunnel was dark and silent and the snowy
gleam at the end seemed very faint but Malina
stumbled on, pulling the Christmas tree and
clutching the glowing red lamp. Soon she was out
in the open again and crossing the high bridge;
she knew that any minute now she'd be able
to hear the train coming.

At last she reached the place she'd chosen. She
was out of breath from running and her hands shook
as she set the Christmas tree alight. The long
flames shooting into the snowy sky were like giant
candles. Malina could clearly hear the train
coming closer now and suddenly there it was, thundering
out of a tunnel, huge clouds of steam bursting around it.

    Then the train driver saw the fire and the waving
lamp. At once he slammed on the emergency brake and
shut off the engine. The whistle screeched. The heavy
train shuddered and shook and slowly, slowly,
gasped to a halt.

Everyone in the train was thrown about. Passengers fell off their seats and luggage crashed to the floor. There was chaos in the restaurant car: waiters, plates, cakes and fish were juggled in the air!

Out in the snow Malina stood quite still, clutching
the glowing lamp and looking up at the huge panting train.
The train driver and the guard jumped out of the
train and ran up to the little girl. "Why, it's Malina!"
exclaimed the driver. "There's a big rockfall in front of the
long tunnel," Malina said, "that's why I had
to stop the train." The two men looked
at each other in astonishment.

Soon everyone on the train had heard about the fall of
rock and how Malina had saved the train. "The child must
be very cold standing out in the snow," someone said
and then Malina found herself being led by the hand into
the restaurant car.

It was very warm in there and Malina looked around to see
lots of strange faces looking down at her. She could tell
that the passengers were discussing something and suddenly
she knew what it was because they were all showering
her with presents!

Then she looked up and saw her father standing in the
carriage doorway, watching. In his arms lay a tiny snow-white
lamb with black spots behind its ears. What a wonderful
Christmas present! Malina jumped up and ran to her father.
"Come on, Daddy, let's go home," she said, "Bella will be
wondering what's happened to us."

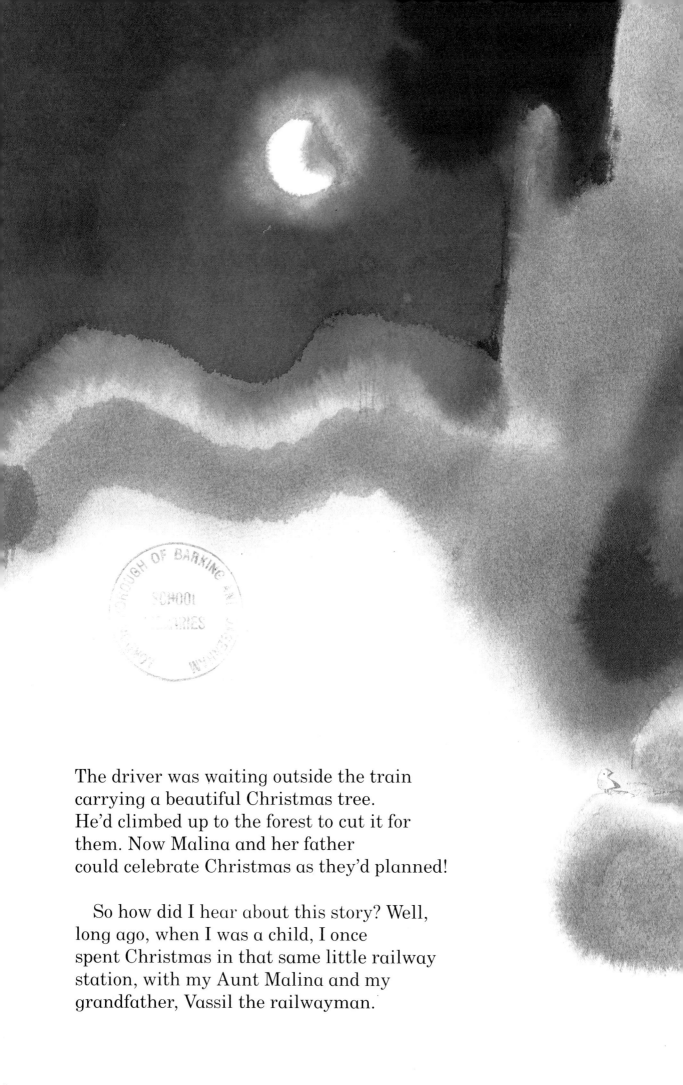

The driver was waiting outside the train
carrying a beautiful Christmas tree.
He'd climbed up to the forest to cut it for
them. Now Malina and her father
could celebrate Christmas as they'd planned!

So how did I hear about this story? Well,
long ago, when I was a child, I once
spent Christmas in that same little railway
station, with my Aunt Malina and my
grandfather, Vassil the railwayman.

VIKING KESTREL

Penguin Books, Harmondsworth, Middlesex, England
Viking Penguin Inc, 40 West 23rd Street, New York, New York 10010, USA
Penguin Books Australia Ltd, Ringwood, Victoria, Australia
Penguin Books Canada Limited, 2801 John Street, Markham, Ontario, Canada L3R 1B4
Penguin Books (NZ) Ltd, 182–190 Wairau Road, Auckland 10, New Zealand

First published by Bohem Press, Zurich, under the title
Der Weihnachtszug 1982
First English edition published in Great Britain by Frederick Warne (Publishers) Ltd 1982
This revised English edition published 1987

Copyright © Bohem Press, Zurich, 1982
English text copyright © Aran John, 1987

British Library Cataloguing in Publication Data information available

ISBN 0-670-81523-3

Printed in Switzerland